With love
to Chris for his support and encouragement,
to Basil, Otis and Lulu for their inspiration,
and to Mum and Dad

First edition for the United States and Canada published by
Barron's Educational Series, Inc., 1999

First published in Great Britain in 1999 by Electric Paper
59 Churchfield Road, London W3 6AY

All inquiries should be addressed to:
Barron's Educational Series, Inc.
250 Wireless Boulevard
Hauppauge, New York 11788
http: / / www.barronseduc.com

ISBN 0-7641-5213-0
Library of Congress Catalog Card No. 99-72572

Manufactured in China
987654321

No More Fleas

Anne Peutrell

BARRON'S

Basil is a very nice cat.
He doesn't mind being
hugged and kissed.

He doesn't mind being used for judo practice

or even when the dog next door uses him as a target.

But there's one thing Basil can't stand...

itchy-scratchy

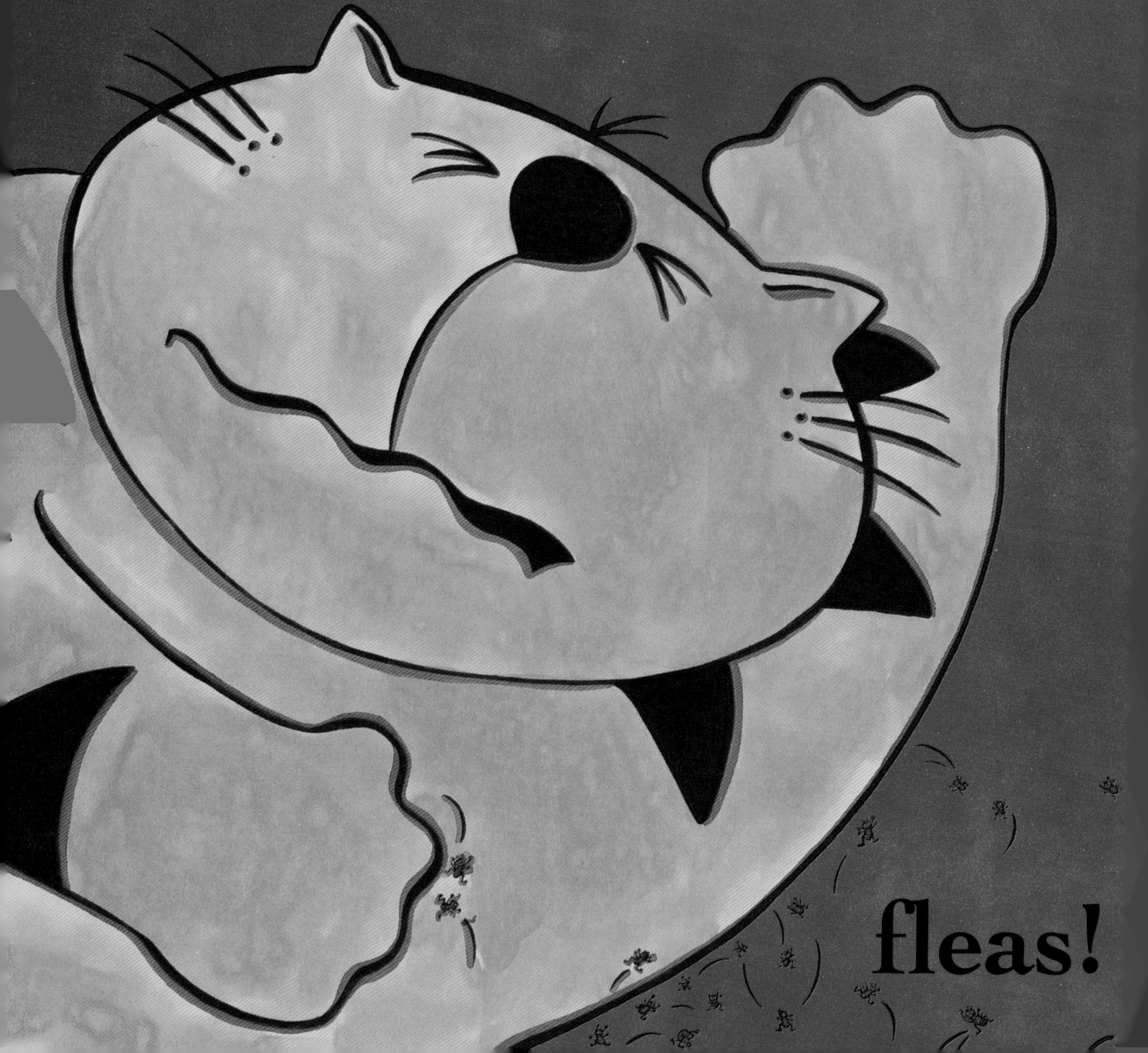

fleas!

Some fleas had made their
home in Basil's furry coat.
They made him itch.
So he scratched.

The more he scratched,
the more he itched.

Basil shouted in a very loud voice,
"FLEAS, PLEASE GO AWAY!"
But they didn't.
"I'll wash them away," cried Basil.

On **Monday**
Basil put on a shower cap,
turned on the water and
rubbed himself with the soap
as hard as possible.

The fleas had fun!

But Basil got soap in his eyes.

"I'll blow them away," thought Basil.

On **Tuesday**

Basil used a hairdryer.

He turned it up to its fastest speed and hottest heat.

The fleas just clung on.
But Basil's hair turned all spikey!

Then he had a great idea.

On **Wednesday**

Basil raided the dressing table.

"Pwaah, this will stink them out!" he exclaimed.

"What a gorgeous smell," shouted the fleas.

Basil's owner was angry.

That night he had to sleep in the garden.

"I'll drive them out," thought Basil.

On **Thursday**

Basil called all his friends.

"We'll form a cat band," he said.

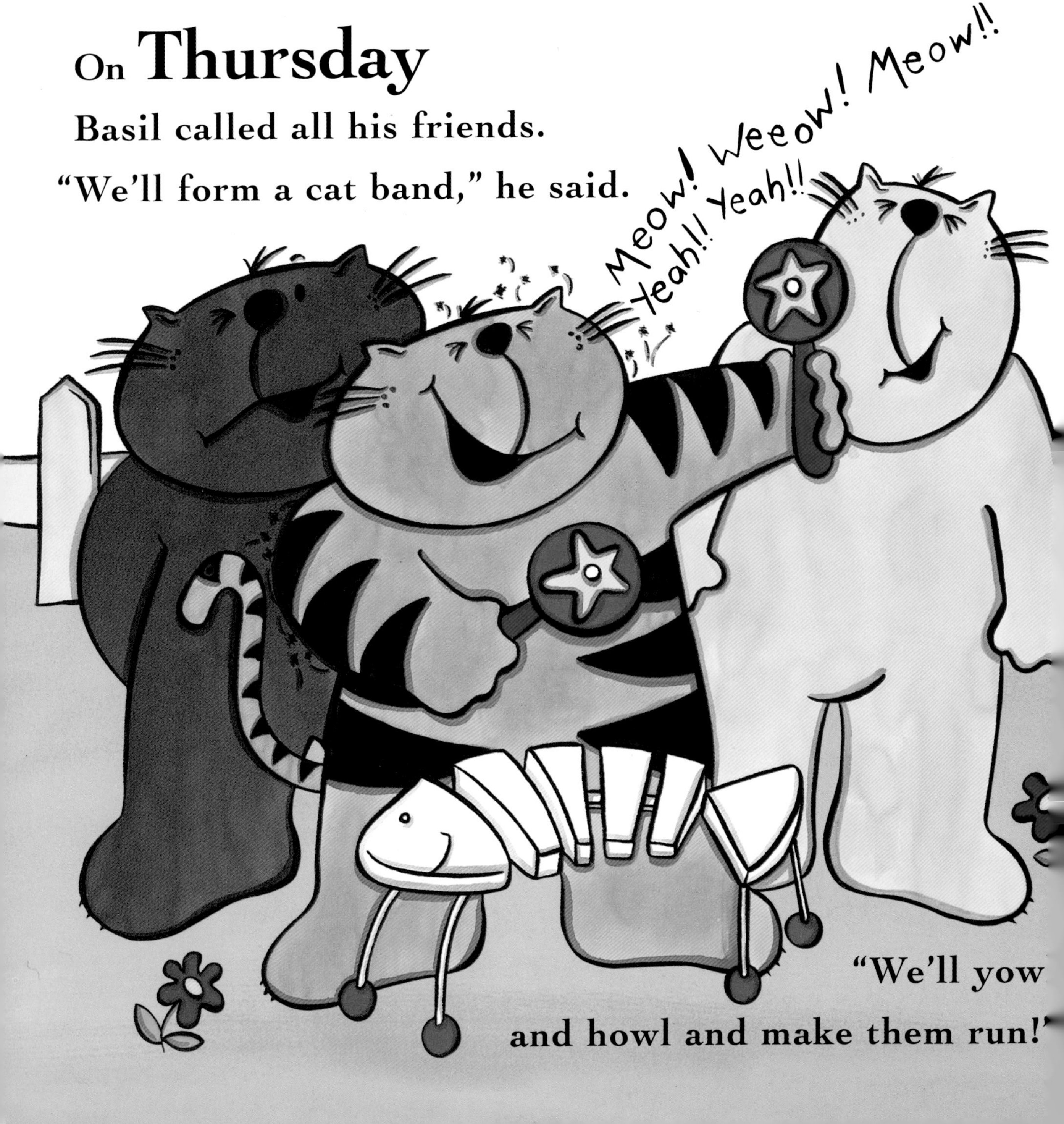
Meow! Weeow! Meow!!
Yeah!! Yeah!!

"We'll yow and howl and make them run!"

But the Fleas had a great time. They jumped and skipped to the music.

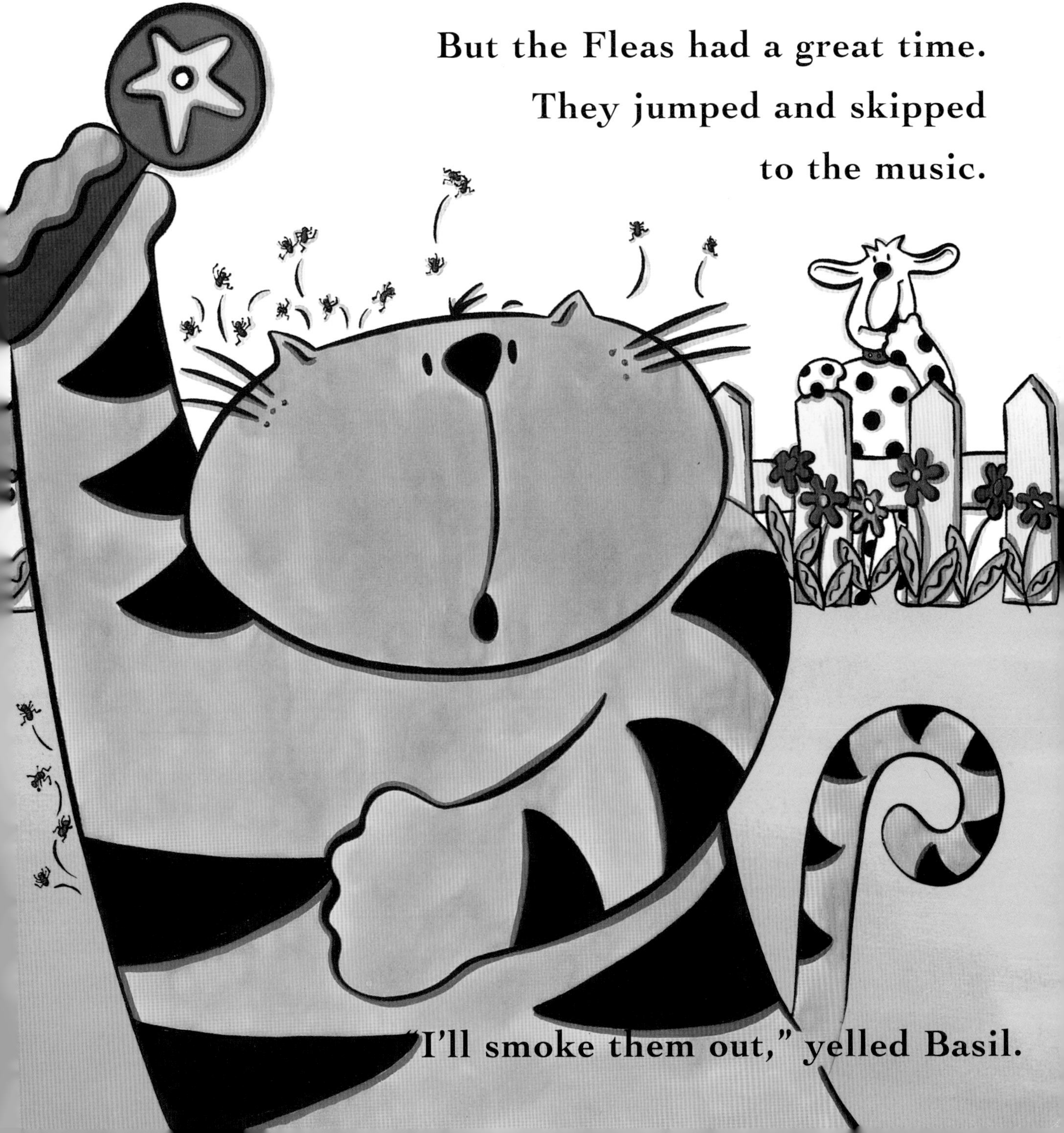

"I'll smoke them out," yelled Basil.

On **Friday**

Basil went up onto the roof and sat on the chimney.
"They'll soon be packing their bags," he chuckled.

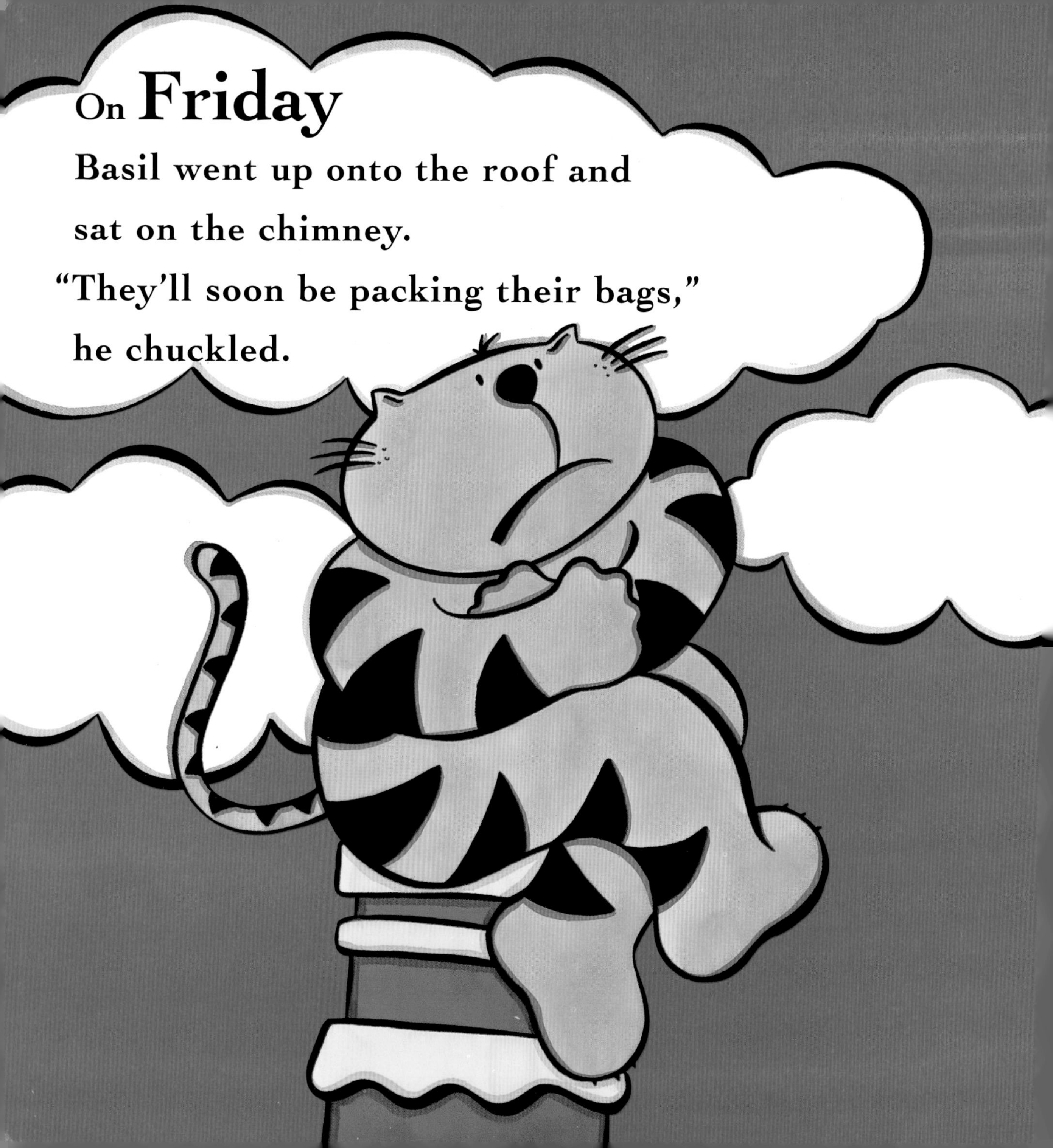

The fleas just buried their noses in Basil's fur.

But Basil couldn't stop coughing.

He needed cheering up, so...

On Saturday

Basil went to the circus.

It was a fantastic show with clowns, tightrope walkers, and jugglers.

The fleas were s
excited they jumped for joy

"FL-EEEE-S PL-EEE-SE STOP JUMPING!"

screamed Basil.

He got thrown out for being too rowdy.

What a catastrophe!

On Sunday

Basil woke up late.

He got ready to scratch.

He got ready to
scratch again.

But there was no itch,
no itch at all,
no itch anywhere.

Then a tiny letter
dropped from behind
Basil's ear.

Dear Cat
We're off to the flea circus to
seek fame and fortune,
ride elephants, swing on
a trapeze, cycle across a
tightrope, travel the
world. Thanks for your
warm hospitality. We
will send you a postcard.
Don't miss us too much.
Lots of love, The Fleas

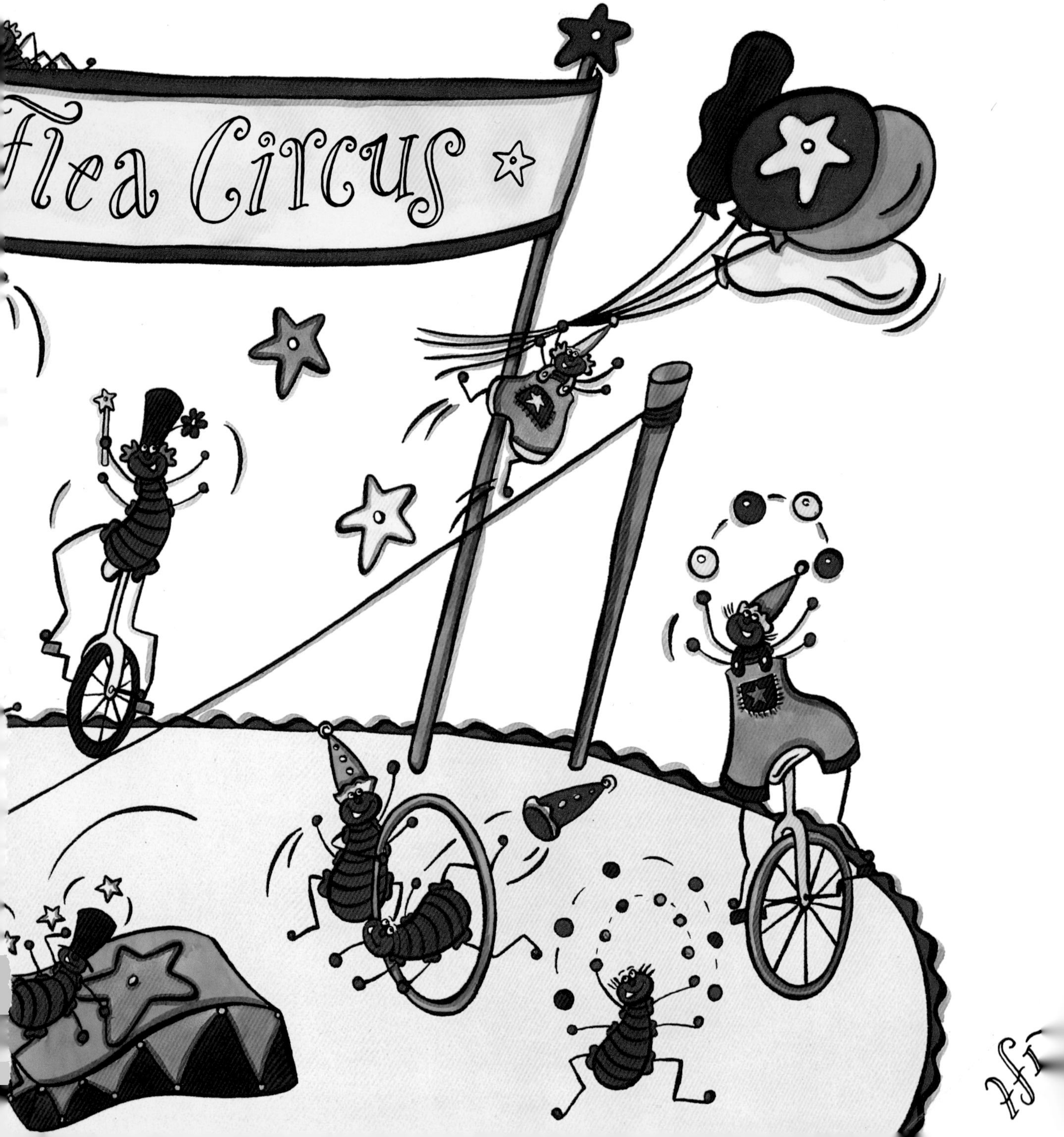
Flea Circus

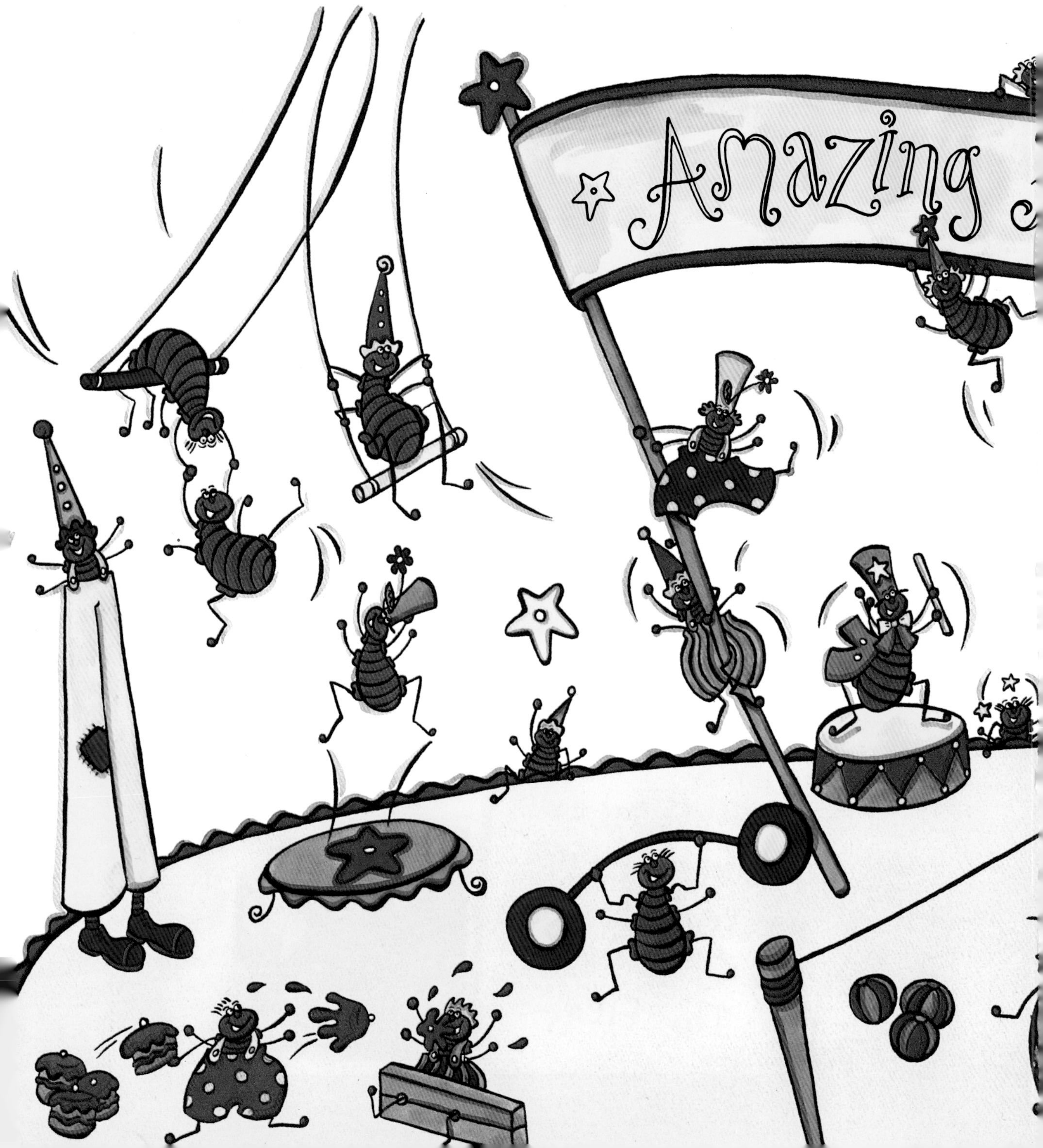
Amazing

A few weeks later,
Basil got a postcard.

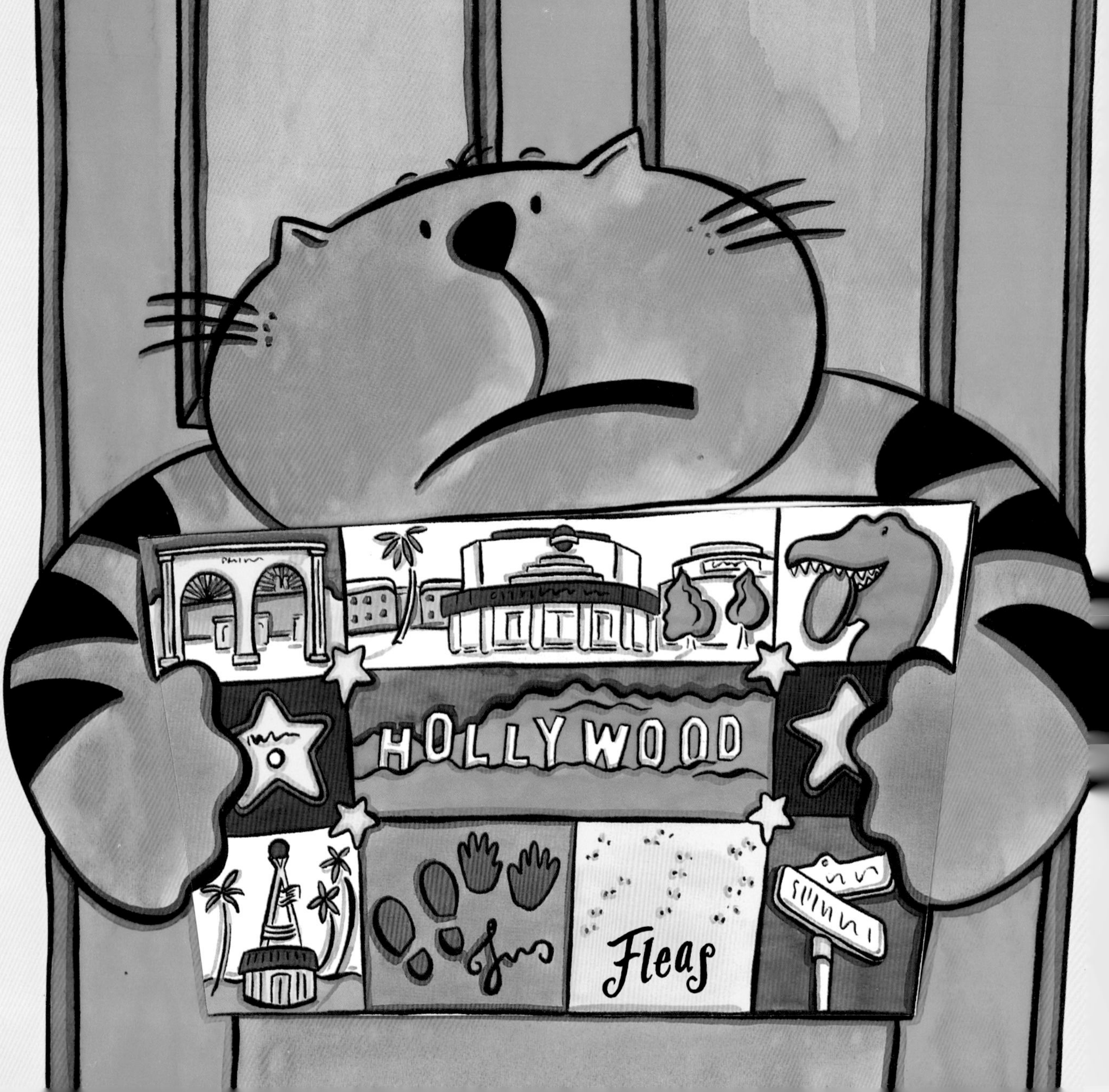
HOLLYWOOD
Fleas

Basil tried to think of ways he could escape from the itchy-scratchy fleas.

He had a brilliant idea!
Basil sent the fleas a postcard.

Soon the fleas came
back home.